DEMON DUSK

Laura Shenton

DEMON DUSK

Laura Shenton

Iridescent Toad Publishing

Iridescent Toad Publishing.

©Laura Shenton 2024
All rights reserved.

Laura Shenton asserts the moral right to be identified as the author of this work.

No part of this publication may be
reproduced, stored or transmitted in any form or by any means, electronic, mechanical, photocopying, recording, scanning, or otherwise without written permission from the publisher. It is illegal to copy this book, post it to a website, or distribute it by any other means without permission.

This book is entirely a work of fiction. The names, characters and incidents portrayed in it are the work of the author's imagination. Any resemblance to actual persons, living or dead, events or localities is entirely coincidental.

Designations used by companies to distinguish their products are often claimed as trademarks. All brand names and product names used in this book and on its cover are trade names, service marks, trademarks and registered trademarks of their respective owners. The publishers and the book are not associated with any product or vendor mentioned in this book. None of the companies referenced within the book have endorsed the book.

Cover by D' Arte Oriel.

First edition. ISBN: 978-1-913779-17-7

Chapter One

Rain hammered down on the glistening streets of Emerald Heights, each droplet slashing through the air before splattering against the cold asphalt. The city's streetlights cast an eerie glow onto the wet pavement, their flickering halos mixing with the darkness as they struggled to keep the shadows at bay.

Ren sprinted, her boots pounding against the slick ground, her breath a series of ragged gasps. Her pink hair clung to her forehead like a soaked mop, and her black leather jacket grew heavier with each step. She could feel the chill seeping into her bones, but she refused to let it slow her down as she charged after the man darting ahead of her.

He weaved in and out of the narrow alleys that crisscrossed the city like a complex labyrinth. Ren cursed under her breath, certain that she was chasing a paranormal.

As she rounded another corner, her thoughts raced. Paranormals were drawn to the city like moths to a flame, and whilst most of them lived openly and harmoniously alongside the non-paranormal population, those with an ulterior motive had to be stopped. It was Ren's job to hunt them down – to protect the innocent and maintain order.

The city's pulse thrummed all around as Ren sprinted, her boots splashing through puddles and her hair whipping against the wind as her target increased his speed.

"Stop!" she shouted, firm and determined. "It's pointless to run!"

Her target glanced back, his eyes locking onto her for a brief moment. He then turned another corner. Ren clenched her teeth, frustration bubbling within as she pushed herself to close the distance between them. Sensing the fear radiating from the man, it fuelled her on.

The rain seemed to fall harder, as if the heavens themselves were attempting to aid

Chapter One

in the capture of Ren's prey. As they rounded another corner into an alleyway, the man stumbled, slipping on a slick patch, courtesy of a discarded pizza box. Seizing her opportunity, Ren moved with lightning-fast speed and quickly cornered the man. With his back facing the wall of a dead end, he had nowhere to run.

"Listen," she said, her voice barely audible above the downpour as she flashed her badge at the man. "I'm a Paranormal Control agent. You've got two options: come willingly, or get your arse handed to you."

"Fuck you," said the man, his thin lips tightening to reveal fangs.

I fucking knew it! Ren thought. *This bastard has bloodthirsty vampire written all over him!*

Ren's boots squelched in the gathering puddles as she took a menacing step forward, her gaze fixed on the vampire's face. He shuddered slightly, betraying his fear, but there was still defiance in his mannerisms.

The vampire snarled, charging towards her. He was fast, but Ren had faced worse than him. She sidestepped his attack, bringing her leg up in a swift kick that took his legs out from beneath him.

"So, you're some righteous little hunter?" he said with a sneer as he looked up at her from the sodden ground, disdain dripping from his words. "You can't arrest me for being a vampire."

"Don't bullshit me," said Ren. "I saw you. You were loitering in that alley behind that club, waiting to pounce on your next victim."

"You can't prove anything."

Suddenly, with a newfound bout of defiance and strength, the vampire grappled with Ren and pulled her to the ground with him. Shoving the heel of her palm up towards his nostrils, she was quickly able to regain her footing.

The vampire got up and lunged at her, his powerful limbs propelling him through the air like a predator closing in on its prey. Ren braced herself, every muscle in her body tensing in anticipation of the impact. Their bodies collided, a tangle of limbs and snarls

Chapter One

as they fought for dominance. The vampire's claws dug into Ren's shoulders, making small puncture marks in her black leather jacket and pressing down on her skin like needles. She gritted her teeth against the pain, her thoughts racing as she searched for an opening to exploit.

"Is that all you've got?" the vampire taunted, his face inches from hers, his breath reeking of iron and decay.

In response, Ren slammed her knee into his groin. The vampire's grip loosened just enough for her to wrench herself free. Quickly re-establishing her composure, she was ready for her opponent. Before he could find his balance, she twisted his arm behind his back and slammed him against the alley's brick wall.

As the vampire struggled against her hold, Ren allowed herself a small, grim smile. If there was one thing that never changed in this twisted world of theirs, it was the satisfaction of proving to these bastards that she wouldn't be fucked with.

"Get off me," the vampire said furiously,

extending his fangs with a malicious click.

His eyes were cold and calculating as he assessed his chances for escape. Suddenly, he leaned in towards Ren's neck.

Adrenaline coursing through her veins, Ren ducked beneath the vampire's arms, her instincts honed to perfection after years of hunting creatures like him.

"Bad move," she whispered, pulling the taser from her pocket and lunging forward to press it against the vampire's side.

Refusing to take any chances, she pulled the trigger. The crackle of electricity filled the air, the sharp odour of ozone mingling with the rain-soaked grime of the alleyway.

The vampire's body convulsed violently, his features contorting in a silent scream of anguish as his muscles locked up. His knees buckled, prompting Ren to catch him before he could hit the ground, an unexpected feeling of pity welling up inside her. She then used the taser to administer a ruthless jab into his side, reminding herself that this creature was a predator, not a victim.

"Let's get you somewhere you can't hurt anyone," she murmured.

As soon as the vampire was able to move, his figure a weakened shadow of his former self, Ren put him in handcuffs and marched him towards the waiting Paranormal Control van parked at the mouth of the alley.

"Hey!" her colleague called out as he emerged from the driver's side of the van. "I heard the commotion. Are you ok?"

"I'm fine, thanks," Ren replied tersely, handing the vampire over. "This bloodsucker was loitering outside one of the clubs, ready to pounce on unsuspecting revellers."

"Good catch," said her colleague, reaching for the van's back door. "We'll get him processed and off the streets."

As Ren helped to secure the vampire in the back of the van, her thoughts drifted back to the alleyway outside the club and the people she had potentially saved tonight. It was a small victory, but it was enough to keep her going, to remind her of why she had chosen this life.

Demon Dusk

Chapter Two

The morning dawn cast a hazy, pink hue over the city, the sun sluggishly creeping up from behind the towering buildings, leaving long, cold shadows in its wake. As the city of Emerald Heights began to stir, Ren headed through the empty streets in the direction of home. Despite her tiredness, she knew she couldn't afford to let her guard down, not even for a moment – but damn, did she crave the comfort of her bed.

"What a night!" she muttered under her breath, stifling a yawn.

With every step, the black leather of her jacket creaked in harmony with the protests of her weary muscles. Her boots, once pristine and polished, now bore the scuffs of the conflict fought and won.

As she approached her apartment building, the faint sound of the city by day started to emerge, the hum of traffic blending with sirens, and distant chatter serving to remind her that the world never slept.

With an exhausted sigh, she pushed open the heavy iron gates and walked wearily across the courtyard. Stepping inside the dimly lit foyer, she was hit by the thick scent of cedarwood. The soft glow of the sconces adorned the walls, casting a warm ambience over the immaculate marble floors. Ren appreciated the meticulous orderliness of the area – each potted plant perfectly placed, and every surface clean and polished.

"Morning, Ren," said the doorman, his familiar voice breaking into her thoughts as he gave a warm smile, his eyes crinkling beneath his bushy white brows. "Long night?"

"Something like that," she replied, forcing a smile on her way to the lift.

"Stay safe out there, kid," he called after her, his voice tinged with concern.

Chapter Two

"Always do," she shot back, the words a promise she couldn't quite bring herself to believe.

She stepped into the lift, its brushed stainless steel doors sliding shut with a hushed whisper. As the lift ascended, her pulse gradually slowed, the familiar rhythm of home settling over her like a well-worn blanket. The pristine marble floors and warm wood panelling spoke of comfort and luxury, but it was the state-of-the-art security system of her apartment that would truly set her heart at ease.

Upon reaching her door, Ren entered the passcodes with practiced precision, the sophisticated alarm system beeping in response to her commands. It was a necessary inconvenience – no Paranormal Control agent could do the job without making a few enemies along the way.

"Home sweet home," she said with a sigh as she pushed open the door and stepped inside.

The soft click of the lock punctuated the quiet space as the door closed behind her, signifying that she could now be at ease. She looked around the room, taking in the familiar scene. It was an oasis of calm amidst the chaos of Emerald Heights. The exposed brick walls and high ceilings gave it an industrial chic feel, whilst the plush furnishings and eclectic artwork in pastel hues with abstract shapes provided serenity and visual interest.

She kicked off her boots and traded them for a pair of worn, comfortable slippers. Padding across the hardwood floor, she shrugged off her black leather jacket and hung it up to dry.

The faint hum of the refrigerator greeted her as she stepped into the kitchen area, a reminder that her life outside of work still existed, even if it felt like a distant memory. She rubbed her temples, trying to shake off the remnants of adrenaline that had fuelled her through yet another intense night shift.

Pulling open the fridge door, she scanned the almost-bare shelves. Her stomach growled audibly, reminding her that she'd been too preoccupied to grab dinner on her way home.

She was relieved to find a small plate with

two slices of cold pizza from the night before, nestled beside a half-empty bottle of cola. It wasn't exactly gourmet fare, but it would do. She hungrily scoffed the pizza, and then washed it down with a large swig of the almost-flat, sweet beverage.

Maybe next time I'll remember to pick up dinner, she thought, a faint smile playing on her lips as she imagined the satisfaction of a full stomach.

Barely satiated, but with little else in the fridge, Ren made her way to the bathroom, her mind already drifting towards the prospect of a hot bath.

As the tub filled with steaming water, Ren caught sight of her reflection in the mirror. The low lighting cast shadows under her eyes, making them look even more tired than usual. The pink strands of hair framing her face were matted with sweat and dried rainwater. Her chapped lips were flaky and sore.

"Damn, I look like shit," she muttered, leaning in closer to examine herself.

She turned off the tap and got undressed, her tired muscles yearning for the heat of the water. She then slipped into the tub, submerging herself up to her neck, feeling the surrounding warmth as it began to soothe her aching body.

"God, that feels good," she murmured, closing her eyes as she let the heat work its magic on her sore limbs.

The tension in her shoulders began to loosen ever so slightly, and for a moment, she allowed herself to forget about the rogue paranormals lurking in the shadows of Emerald Heights.

"Wow, I needed this," she said breathily, taking in the calming atmosphere.

Surrendering herself to the gentle embrace of the liquid cocoon, she felt the tension melt away. Her fingers traced the edge of the ceramic tub, her ears filled by the sound of water sloshing softly against the sides. It was a stark contrast to the mayhem of a typical night shift. The quietude lulled her mind, and she found herself drifting towards sleep.

Chapter Two

Shit! I'd better not fall asleep in here.

With a reluctant sigh, she carefully rose from the bath and stepped out onto a soft mat, rivulets of water cascading down her body. She reached for a fluffy towel and wrapped it around herself, welcoming its comforting touch.

Padding into her bedroom, still damp from the bath, she craved the mattress and the cool touch of the sheets. She then took one last swig of cola from a half-empty bottle that she'd left by her bedside, knowing full well that making a cup of tea would be too much effort in her exhausted state.

As she nestled under the covers, the sounds of the waking city drifted through her window: the distant scrape of shutters opening, the thrum of pedestrians on their way to work, and the faint song of an early bird.

As drowsiness took its hold on her, a faint smile touched Ren's lips as she reflected on the night's victories and found solace in her determination to keep the city and its residents safe.

Demon Dusk

Chapter Three

The fluorescent office lights of Paranormal Control flickered overhead as Ren surveyed the cluttered room. She leaned against her desk, tapping her fingers impatiently on the worn surface. A career of chasing things that went bump in the night had sharpened her senses, and she could feel the tension in the air, like an electric current running just beneath her skin.

"Here you go, Ren," said Amy, handing her a steaming cup of coffee. "I figured we'd need this for the briefing tonight."

With her short, spiky black hair, and with tattoo sleeves adorning her arms, Ren's colleague fitted right into the gritty world they both inhabited.

"Thanks, Amy," Ren said with a grateful smile. "You know me well."

Ren took a sip of the dark, rich brew. It was perfect – just how she liked it. Over the years, she had worked closely with Amy on a number of vital cases. They weren't just colleagues; they were friends, bound by their shared experiences and unyielding dedication to keeping Emerald Heights safe from paranormal threats.

"Someone's got to look after you," Amy teased, using her elbow to give Ren a playful nudge.

Amy's expression was a mixture of warmth and mischief, belying the tough exterior she presented to the world. Beneath that layer of armour, was a woman who cared deeply for those in need and sought to protect the innocent at all costs.

"Alright, alright," Ren said, rolling her eyes but unable to suppress a grin. "Let's get our arses over to this briefing."

As they made their way towards the conference room, Ren couldn't help but worry about what new horrors awaited them. The past few weeks had been particularly brutal, with two young women having been found murdered under mysterious circumstances. Emerald Heights wasn't exactly a haven of peace and tranquillity, but something about these deaths felt different – darker.

The conference room buzzed with an anxious energy, casting a pall over the Paranormal Control agents as they took their seats. Ren settled into her chair, her gaze fixed on the projector screen at the front of the room. Beside her, Amy leaned back in her chair, arms crossed, tattoos on full display beneath the fluorescent lights.

"Alright, everyone," their boss – Brent Statham – announced, his firm baritone commanding the space as he swiftly clapped his hands. "Let's get started."

The respected leader of Paranormal Control looked out at his team, exuding calmness and authority despite the dark rings beneath his eyes. Ren knew that he, like them, had been working tirelessly to keep the city safe from unscrupulous paranormals.

"Unfortunately," Statham began, "we have another case on our hands; a third body has been discovered."

"Shit," Ren murmured under her breath.

"Has the victim been identified?" a colleague asked from the back of the room.

"Yes," Statham replied, clicking a button on the remote to reveal an image of the victim on the screen. "Lyndall Charwood: another young woman, found by the edge of Lake Seraphim – just like the previous two."

Ren's heart sank as she studied Lyndall's face – another innocent life snuffed out, another family shattered. She exchanged a sombre glance with Amy before focusing her attention back to Statham.

"Lyndall's death shares several characteristics with the cases of Candice Bundy and Samantha Redwood," he said.

He clicked through a series of images with disturbing similarities. The three victims were all females in their early twenties, their bodies left by the water, marked by violence

Chapter Three

and terror.

Ren clenched her jaw and honed in on the grisly details before her, pushing away the gut-wrenching sorrow that threatened to swallow her whole.

"Fucking hell," Amy muttered, rubbing a hand over her face. "This is getting out of control."

As the agents absorbed the grim news, Ren felt a knot of dread tightening in her stomach. She couldn't shake the feeling that they were dealing with something deeply sinister.

"Any leads on who or what might be behind this?" someone asked.

"Nothing concrete yet," Statham admitted, his brow creasing in frustration. "We need to find the connection between these victims and determine what kind of paranormal we're up against. Ren and Amy, I want you to lead the investigation."

"Of course," said Ren, her voice firm, and her mind racing with possibilities.

"Everyone else," said Statham, "I need you out on street patrol. We can't afford to let our guard down while this killer is still out there."

"Too right," said a stern-looking woman seated at the side of the room.

"Alright, everyone," Statham concluded. "We've got our work cut out for us. Let's get to it."

As the other agents filed out of the room, Ren caught Amy's eye, the weight of their task settling heavily upon their shoulders as they remained seated, waiting for further instructions.

"Ren, Amy, I want you to visit the morgue tonight," Statham asserted, addressing them with a determined gaze. "Dr Carmichael should have finished his examination of the body by now. Go and see what he's found."

"Understood," Ren said with a resolute nod.

She felt a shiver run down her spine at the thought of examining the brutalised remains of Lyndall Charwood. It was a necessary part of the job, but that didn't make it any less unsettling.

"Good luck," Statham said, patting them on the shoulders as they prepared to leave. "And remember, whatever you find, keep me informed."

"Will do," Amy promised.

Demon Dusk

Chapter Four

As they exited the offices of Paranormal Control, Ren couldn't help but feel a chill that had nothing to do with the night air.

"Are we ready for this?" Amy asked quietly, her voice betraying a hint of nervousness.

"About as ready as we'll ever be," Ren replied stoically.

They climbed into an unmarked vehicle, the city lights reflecting off the tinted windows. With Ren in the front passenger seat, Amy drove as they sat in silence for a moment, lost in their thoughts and mentally preparing themselves for the morgue. The low hum of the car's engine provided an almost soothing counterpoint to the tension that hung in the air.

"God, I hate going to the morgue," Amy muttered, her knuckles turning white as she gripped the steering wheel a little tighter. "It always feels so... final."

"Same here," Ren replied, her voice steady despite the unease she felt at the thought of examining the victim.

The city's neon lights rippled across the black surface of the unmarked car, casting a kaleidoscope of colours over Ren and Amy as they continued their drive through Emerald Heights. As they neared their destination, the buildings seemed to loom ever larger.

Soon enough, they pulled up outside the morgue, its sterile façade offering no hint of the horrors that lay within its walls.

"Ready?" Amy asked.

"Never," Ren admitted with a wry smile. "But let's get this over with."

Exiting the vehicle, they approached the morgue, steeling themselves for the bleak task ahead. The cold air prickled their skin. A stark contrast to the heated interior of the

Chapter Four

car, it served as a chilling reminder of the lifeless body that awaited them inside.

The building's doors groaned open, revealing a dimly lit corridor that seemed to swallow all warmth. Ren shivered involuntarily as they stepped inside, the frigidity of the place seeping into her bones. The scent of disinfectant mingled with a faint, metallic tang, creating an unsettling odour that clung to the back of her throat.

As they ventured further into the building, the oppressive atmosphere seemed to thicken around them, closing in from all sides like a suffocating embrace. The low hum of powerful refrigeration units filled the air, punctuated by the occasional distant echo of a dripping tap.

"Dr Carmichael?" Ren called out, her voice sounding feeble in the vast clinical space.

"Over here," came a gravelly reply, emanating from a small room just off the main corridor.

Ren and Amy followed the sound to find the forensic pathologist stood over a steel table. The harsh fluorescent lights cast stark shadows across his face, emphasising the deep lines etched into his weathered features.

"Good evening, Dr Carmichael," Ren greeted him with a nod, trying her best to sound professional despite the churning unease in her stomach.

"Ms Cain," he said, addressing Ren before turning to greet Amy. "Ms Carver."

His gaze lingered for a moment on Ren's pink hair, but he soon returned his focus to the task at hand.

"You're here about the Charwood woman, I presume?"

"That's right," said Ren, her eyes flicking briefly to the concealed body on the table before her. "We need your expert opinion on her injuries."

"Of course," said Dr Carmichael, his demeanour suggesting that he had seen far too many such cases in his time. "I must warn you though, it isn't pretty."

Chapter Four

"We've seen the photos," Amy interjected, her tone resolute.

"Very well," said Dr Carmichael.

He carefully peeled back the sheet to reveal Lyndall Charwood's lifeless body. Ren clenched her jaw, willing herself not to look away as she took in the gruesome sight. The victim's skin was marred with dark bruises and long, jagged scratches that seemed to cover every inch of her. Her limbs were twisted at unnatural angles, as if she had been tortured before death.

"Jesus," Amy muttered under her breath as she studied the injuries. "This is dreadful."

"Indeed," Dr Carmichael agreed, his tone solemn. "I've seen my fair share of violence, but this... this is extreme."

"Any idea what could've done this?" Ren asked, trying to keep her voice steady.

She couldn't help but feel a pang of empathy for the poor woman – whoever had killed her had clearly wanted her to suffer.

"Take a closer look at the nature of these wounds," he said, gesturing towards the body. "The absence of certain marks speaks volumes. We know she suffered, but there are no fang marks on the neck. It's definitely not the work of a vampire. You can rule out shifters too – there are no telltale bite marks to be found."

Ren furrowed her brow, absorbing the details under the sterile lights.

"So, not a vampire or a shifter," she confirmed. "What are we dealing with here?"

"The scratches on her body suggest a different kind of predator," asserted Dr Carmichael, a hint of sadness shadowing his expression. "Witches, mages, perhaps even a demon – they're going to be your most likely suspects."

"Wait," Amy said urgently, pointing to something on Lyndall's palm.

Ren leaned in closer, her eyes widening as she spotted the small, intricate mark etched into the woman's skin. It looked almost like a brand, its lines forming a sinister, swirling pattern.

Chapter Four

"What's that?" she asked.

"I recognise that symbol," said Amy. "It's connected to a demon nightclub – Infernal Decadence."

"Are you sure?" Ren asked.

"Positive," Amy confirmed. "I've seen it before. Infernal Decadence is located on the affluent outskirts of the city, but don't let that fool you. It's not necessarily high-end. It's an underground club, so I have no idea if it's pleasant or more of a run-down and rough kind of place."

"There's only one way to find out," said Ren, her mind racing with possibilities. "This lead could be the key to solving not just Lyndall's murder, but maybe even the cases of Candice Bundy and Samantha Redwood. We need to go and check it out."

"I agree," said Amy.

"Thanks for your help," Ren said, her tone sincere as she addressed Dr Carmichael.

A welcome reprieve from the suffocating

atmosphere, the relative cleanliness of the night air surrounded Ren and Amy as they stepped out of the morgue. Ren took a deep breath, filling her lungs with the crisp freshness. It was a small comfort, but one she savoured. Trying to shake off the lingering image of the victim from her mind, she adjusted her black leather jacket, tugging at the collar.

"Let's get back to headquarters," she said. "We need to do our research before setting foot in that club."

"Right," Amy agreed, her tone supportive and certain.

As they climbed into their unmarked vehicle, Ren couldn't help but feel a sense of urgency settling over her. With each passing moment, the killer was still out there, free to strike again.

Chapter Five

The dull hum of strip lighting filled the air as Ren and Amy trudged back into the building of Paranormal Control, their boots echoing against the cold linoleum floor. As soon as they got to the office, they shrugged off their jackets, wincing at the lingering stench of death that seemed to cling to them like a second skin.

"God, I need a shower," Amy muttered, tossing her gloves onto the desk with a disgusted expression.

Ren nodded in agreement, running a hand through her vibrant pink hair, leaving it in disarray.

"Later," she said, powering up her computer, her features a picture of resolve. "We've got work to do."

Amy sighed as she took a seat beside Ren and opened the case files on her own computer. The gruesome images of Lyndall Charwood, Samantha Redwood, and Candice Bundy dominated the screens, their lifeless eyes forever frozen in terror. Ren frowned, her fingers drumming impatiently on the desk as she scanned the reports.

"Something's not adding up," she mused aloud, her expression creasing with frustration. "Why leave the bodies at the edge of the lake? Why not dump them in the water?"

"Maybe our murderer got cold feet?" Amy suggested, though her tone was doubtful. "Hmm... I'm not sure though. Leaving the bodies at the edge of the water? It seems too... deliberate."

"Exactly," said Ren, leaning back in her chair, her eyes narrowing as she tapped the end of a pen against her chin. "And that mark on Charwood's palm: it links her to Infernal Decadence. But how?"

"Let's see if the other victims had ties with that place," Amy offered, already pulling up

Chapter Five

their social media profiles.

She clicked through photos, status updates, and friend lists with practiced efficiency, searching for any mention of the demon nightclub.

"Nothing on Redwood," she reported after several minutes of fruitless scrolling. "And Bundy... Nope, not a damn thing."

"Shit," Ren cursed. "What are we missing?"

"Maybe it's not as obvious as we think," Amy said, rubbing her temples, her tattooed arms flexing with the motion.

"Or maybe..." said Ren, her eyes suddenly widening as an idea formed in her mind. "Maybe it's something they kept hidden – something that only someone close to them would know."

"Like a secretive connection to Infernal Decadence?" said Amy, intrigued by Ren's theory.

"Exactly," said Ren. "We need to find out if there's anyone who knew all three of the victims. Let's dig deeper into Infernal Decadence."

Ren kept her eyes on the screen as she typed furiously at the keyboard. The quiet hum of the computer was drowned out by the click-clack of keys.

Pulling up several different windows on her own screen, Amy scoured the internet for any information about the nightclub.

"I think... wait, I've found something."

"Spill it," Ren demanded, glancing over at Amy's screen.

"It looks like Infernal Decadence is owned by someone named Charles Bosgrove," Amy revealed.

"Charles Bosgrove..." Ren mused, her pink hair shifting as she shook her head. "The name doesn't ring a bell. Let's check our files."

She navigated to the Paranormal Control database and typed in the name, keenly anticipating the search results.

Chapter Five

"Nope," Ren muttered, frustration evident in her tone. "He's not in our system. How the hell is an owner of a demon nightclub not on our radar?"

"Maybe we just haven't crossed paths with him yet," said Amy.

"Either way, we need to find out more about this guy," Ren said, her jaw set with certainty. "That mark on Charwood's palm: it's not the sort of thing that a person just casually gets. If Infernal Decadence is linked to these murders, then we at least need to check out the owner of the club to get a sense of what we might be dealing with here."

"I agree," said Amy.

"Right," said Ren. "We need to find out whether Bosgrove himself is a demon. We can't just barge into Infernal Decadence without knowing what we're walking into."

"True," said Amy, scanning the information on the screen once more. "We need to gather as much intel as we can before making our next move."

Amy's gaze remained fixed on the monitor. Her pupils traced the contours of the screen with unwavering commitment.

"Hey, look at this," she said urgently, pointing to a forum post discussing demons and their influence in the city. "Someone here claims that Charles Bosgrove is a demon."

"Let's see what else we can find," Ren replied, her fingers flying across her own keyboard.

As more information began to surface, it became clear that the owner of Infernal Decadence was indeed a demon.

"Damn, he's slick," Amy muttered, scrolling through images of Bosgrove that had been uploaded by others. "No wonder he's managed to keep such a low profile."

From the photos, Bosgrove looked to be in his mid-thirties. Suited and booted, often with a glass of champagne in his hand, his polished appearance oozed wealth and sophistication. His undeniable charisma shone through the screen. He clearly had the ability to draw people to him like moths to a flame.

Chapter Five

"Tomorrow night, we're going to Infernal Decadence," Ren stated firmly. "We need to observe Bosgrove, see who he's interacting with, and gather as much intel as we can."

"Sounds good to me," Amy agreed.

Demon Dusk

Chapter Six

Ren stared at her reflection in her bedroom's full-length mirror, adjusting her tight black vest over her dark jeans and smoothing down her signature pink hair. She pursed her lips as she applied another layer of dark lipstick, trying to perfect her look for the night ahead. From her research, Infernal Decadence was notorious for attracting a mixed crowd of demons and non-paranormals alike. Regardless, blending in would be crucial if she and Amy were to find any leads on Lyndall Charwood's murder.

You've got this, she told herself as she fastened the clasp on the black lace choker around her neck.

Ren and Amy had decided to go to the club separately. They reasoned that by walking in alone and meeting on the dance floor, it would help to maintain their cover; they couldn't afford to raise suspicion. Travelling alone would make them less likely to be identified as a team, and would give them a better chance to gather information independently en route.

"Showtime," Ren murmured, slipping into her black leather jacket.

She sent Amy a quick text to say she was on her way, and then pocketed her phone as she made her way out of her apartment door.

***

Ren's boots echoed on the pavement as she ventured deeper into the affluent end of Emerald Heights. The contrasting darkness of the night and the subtle glow of streetlights cast haunting shadows around her. Following her instincts, she searched for any discreet clues that would lead her to the elusive underground nightclub.

Scanning the area for any signs, she eventually spotted a faded arrow painted on a brick wall. It was almost invisible, but still distinctive enough.

Chapter Six

Bingo!

Her heart pounded with anticipation as she descended the narrow, graffiti-covered staircase leading to the entrance of Infernal Decadence. The muffled thump of bass reverberating from within the club hinted at what awaited her inside.

Bracing herself and trying to look unfazed, she opened the heavy steel door to find herself enveloped in a cacophony of blasting techno music and rapidly blinking strobe lights that seemed to pierce through her very core. She felt as if she had been thrust into a vortex of sound and colour, each beat of the bass vibrating against her chest.

To her surprise, the atmosphere of the club was not quite what she had been expecting. Instead of the ostentatious displays of wealth and debauchery that she had envisioned, Infernal Decadence appeared to be much like any other average nightclub.

The walls were adorned with the usual combination of neon signs and urban art. The patrons seemed more interested in enjoying their night out than flaunting their status or causing trouble. The dance floor was packed with writhing bodies, their movements synchronised to the hypnotic rhythm. Booths along the far wall were full of clubbers engaged in intimate conversations and raucous laughter, each group seemingly oblivious to the others.

This isn't as bad as I thought it would be.

As Ren navigated through the heaving dance floor, her eyes darted around, carefully analysing the crowd. She noticed both demons and non-paranormals mingling together, smiling as they danced. It was a relief to know that she and Amy wouldn't stand out too much among the diverse clientele.

Maybe we'll actually have some fun tonight, she thought, allowing herself a fleeting moment of hope before her focus returned to their mission. She then discretely scanned the room for any signs of Charles Bosgrove.

Nothing yet.

The dance floor was packed, every inch occupied by dancers lost in the rhythm and

Chapter Six

their own carnal desires. Ren wove her way through the throng of people, searching for Amy. She soon spotted her colleague, her short, spiky black hair bobbing to the beat of the music as she moved effortlessly; she seemed at ease in this environment. Ren wasn't surprised. She had seen Amy party off-shift. Ren admired how easily Amy could switch between roles; tonight, she was undercover, and she played the part flawlessly.

"Hey!" Ren shouted, catching Amy's attention above the din of the club and moving to speak into her ear. "What do you want to drink?"

"Vodka and orange!" Amy yelled back.

As Ren pushed her way towards the bar, she marvelled at Amy's ability to seamlessly navigate the revelry with genuine enthusiasm. Although consuming alcohol on the job would be less than ideal, Ren recognised the tactical advantage in Amy's decision to embrace their undercover façade. It also meant that she could order something plain for herself without arousing suspicion.

"Vodka and orange, and an orange juice, please," she ordered, her voice firm against the pounding music.

She tried to keep her focus on the bartender, but couldn't resist glancing around the room, taking in the flickering shadows created by the massive ornamental flames and red strip lighting behind the bar.

"Coming right up," the bartender said with a polite nod before turning to make the drinks.

As Ren waited, she allowed her gaze to wander over the sea of faces all around, her instincts on high alert for any sign of danger or deceit. Suddenly, to her surprise, she spotted Charles Bosgrove across the room. He was holding court amongst a group of fawning admirers. He seemed to exude an air of dark magnetism that drew people in. The flickering lights cast shadows across his chiselled features. Cradling a tumbler in his hand, he swirled the amber liquid within as he spoke.

Ren couldn't help but be struck by his physical presence – he was even more stunning in the flesh than in his photos. His powerful aura was both captivating and unnerving, yet the members of his entourage seemed to hang on his every word with great respect.

"Here you go," said the bartender, placing the drinks down in front of Ren.

"Thanks," she said, handing him a couple of notes. "Keep the change."

Not wishing to lose sight of Bosgrove, Ren swiftly weaved through the crowd back to Amy.

"He's here," she announced as she handed over the vodka and orange.

"I see him," said Amy.

Their focus divided between maintaining their cover and keeping a discreet-but-frequent gaze on their target, Ren and Amy continued to exploit the dance floor as their stage, each movement calculated to facilitate their aims and keep their true purpose veiled.

Demon Dusk

Chapter Seven

Amidst the pulsating throb of the dance floor, as Ren and Amy continued their rhythmic sway, their gaze deviated subtly between the revellers surrounding them, and Bosgrove at the other end of the bar.

Suddenly, a song came on that transformed the club's atmosphere into a heightened frenzy of movement. The crowd, already lost in the rhythm, responded with an infectious fervour. As the track reached its climax, a collective euphoria swept over the dance floor. Arms shot skywards, creating a flurry of raised hands that moved with the undulating melody. The energy surged through the crowd like a current, a communal expression of joy that transcended the boundaries of individual movements.

Ren's heart quickened, a silent realisation shooting through her as she spotted a particular set of raised hands. One of the palms bore exactly the same distinctive mark as the one she had observed on Lyndall Charwood's lifeless palm.

Lowering her gaze to locate the owner of the hands, Ren's eyes caught the hypnotic sway of long emerald-green hair on a young woman. She twirled gracefully, her locks creating an ephemeral curtain that flowed seductively with every spirited movement.

Unable to shout the details to Amy without blowing their cover, Ren fumbled in her pocket for her phone. She whipped it out and then typed a quick message:

Female, green hair, dark jeans, white vest. Mark on palm. I'm on her. Keep watch on Bosgrove.

Amy's phone vibrated, causing her to grab it and read the message with a swift glance. She then gave Ren a nod of confirmation.

Ren hesitated for a moment, assessing the atmosphere on the dance floor. As it

Chapter Seven

thrummed with vibrance and camaraderie, she decided it was safe to approach the green-haired woman without arousing suspicion.

Pretending to enjoy herself whilst swinging her hips in time with the beat, Ren danced her way closer to the woman.

"Hey! I love your pink hair!" the woman shouted over the music, grinning at Ren.

"Thanks! Yours is pretty awesome too!" Ren replied, trying to appear relaxed as they danced together.

Now that Ren was closer to the woman, she could sense that she wasn't a paranormal of any kind. The two continued to dance among the other club-goers, gradually growing more comfortable with each other.

Suddenly, the green-haired woman gestured to her friends that she was going to head out for a smoke. Ren knew that she had to seize this opportunity.

"Mind if I join you?" Ren shouted above the music.

"Of course not!" the woman replied. "Let's go."

As the woman exited the club and made her way up the stairs, she explored her pockets for a lighter. A good few paces behind, Ren observed that she seemed to be sober – or at least certainly close to it.

Once outside, the cool night air hit Ren like a refreshing wave, a stark contrast to the heat and humidity of the club. The green-haired woman lit a cigarette, while Ren pulled out her own pack, silently cursing herself for having to participate in this unhealthy habit just for the sake of her cover. As the woman offered Ren a light, their conversation began to flow more naturally.

"God, I've been needing this," the woman admitted, exhaling a long puff of smoke into the night sky.

"Me too," Ren lied, her mind racing as she worked to look cool and laidback. "I haven't been here before, but Infernal Decadence seems like a fun place."

"I've been coming here for years," the woman

replied, seemingly oblivious to Ren's ulterior motives. "I guess you could say I'm a regular. I even got the club's mark put on my palm."

She held up her hand, showing off the intricate symbol.

"Wow, you must really love this place," said Ren, feigning shock. "I thought that mark had some deeper meaning behind it."

The woman laughed, shaking her head as she flicked the ash off the end of her cigarette.

"Nah, it's just free advertising for the club," she said. "I wear their mark, and in exchange, I get free drinks for life."

The woman took one last drag of her cigarette and then stubbed it out under her boot.

"You're mad," Ren said jokingly, keen to appear lighthearted.

"Maybe," said the woman, a smirk tugging at her lips. "By the way, I'm Erin."

Before Ren could say anything else, a pair of

young women approached, intent on heading down the stairs and into the nightclub. However, Erin quickly stepped forward, blocking their path.

"Sorry, but you two aren't welcome here," she stated firmly, her voice cold and unyielding. "You'd better fuck off somewhere else."

The two women exchanged glances, sizing up Ren as she stood next to Erin. Evidently deciding it wasn't worth the trouble, they turned on their heels and crossed the street in search of another destination.

Ren couldn't hide her surprise at Erin's sudden display of toughness. As the two young women disappeared into the night, she turned to Erin, her curiosity piqued.

"Who were they?" Ren asked, trying to keep her tone casual.

"Banshees," Erin replied, her voice carrying an edge of bitterness. "I can't stand them – especially after what happened to those poor women who were murdered."

Ren's heart skipped a beat. This was exactly

the sort of information she had been hoping to find while undercover. She quickly masked her enthusiasm with a casual shrug, and offered Erin another cigarette whilst starting another one of her own.

"You think they had something to do with it?"

"I might be wrong," said Erin, lighting her cigarette, "but Lyndall was in another class at the university with me. When she started hanging out with the banshees, we saw less and less of her. And then, well, everyone knows what happened after that."

Ren frowned, thinking about how she and Amy had never encountered banshees during their work for Paranormal Control.

"There aren't many banshees around here, are there?"

"Right," Erin confirmed. "They're part of some exchange programme from a paranormal academy out of town. But I don't like them. Something about them doesn't add up."

"Maybe you're being a bit irrational?" Ren suggested, keen to test the waters without pushing too hard.

"Maybe," Erin conceded, looking thoughtful.

Ren couldn't shake the feeling that she was onto something big. First though, she needed more information before making any rash decisions.

"Who knows," she said with a sigh, stubbing out her cigarette and offering a sympathetic smile. "Life's pretty crazy sometimes, isn't it?"

"Tell me about it," Erin agreed, her expression betraying a hint of sadness.

With a shiver, Ren pulled her black leather jacket tighter around herself, the cold night air seeping through to her bones.

"Let's head back inside," she said. "I'm freezing my arse off out here."

"Sounds good to me," said Erin, stubbing the rest of her cigarette out on a nearby handrail.

They descended the stairs back into Infernal

Decadence. Once they reached the dance floor, Erin rejoined her friends, all seemingly unfazed by the dark undercurrents running beneath their city.

Ren scanned the crowd, finally spotting Amy across the room. Weaving her way through the writhing mass of dancers, Ren sidled up to Amy and raised an eyebrow in question. Amy merely shook her head and shrugged, indicating that nothing noteworthy had happened with Bosgrove during Ren's absence.

As the bass thudded against her chest, Ren decided that perhaps they needed to shift their focus elsewhere.

"Come on," she shouted to Amy above the blaring music, gesturing towards the exit.

Amy nodded, and the two of them made their way out of Infernal Decadence, leaving the throbbing music and sweaty bodies behind. With a new lead to follow, the night was far from over.

***

At Paranormal Control, the door to the office swung open. Ren strode in with Amy following closely behind, their steps muffled by the industrial carpeting that covered the floor. The quiet office was a stark contrast to the constant bass of Infernal Decadence.

Ren's mind raced like a wild horse as she thought back to her encounter with Erin. She had eagerly shared every detail of it with Amy on their way back from the club, riding in an unmarked vehicle driven by one of their colleagues.

"Alright," Ren said, slamming her hands down on the desk and leaning forward, her pink hair falling over her face. "We need to focus on the banshees now."

"Agreed," Amy replied, her tattooed arms crossed over her chest as she thoughtfully tapped a pen against her mouth. "There's so much we don't know about them. We've certainly got our work cut out on the research front."

"Yeah," Ren conceded as she sat down in front of her computer.

Chapter Seven

Her fingers flew across the keyboard as she began to search for information while Amy did the same on a separate machine. They worked in focused silence, their eyes scanning web pages and articles for any clues that could help them in understanding the nature of banshees.

Finally, a surprised gasp escaped Amy's lips as she stumbled upon a crucial piece of information.

"Ren, listen to this," she said urgently, tapping the screen. "It says here that banshees must stay out of water because it would cause them to burn to death."

"Shit," Ren muttered, absorbing the significance of this fact. "Perhaps that's why the bodies were found near the lake, but not in the water! It makes sense!"

"Exactly," Amy agreed. "If a banshee is behind the murders, it explains why they didn't dump the bodies into Lake Seraphim; they couldn't risk getting too close to the water."

"Damn, we might be onto something here," Ren said, her mind churning with possibilities. "Now that we know banshees are in the frame, we need to figure out our next move."

Amy nodded as she leaned in closer to her computer screen.

"Right," she said. "We need to learn more about their habits and weaknesses. We could also do with more information on this exchange programme that they're apparently on. We need to know *exactly* what brought them to Emerald Heights in the first place."

"Definitely," Ren agreed. "Let's dig deeper."

As they delved further into the world of banshees, Ren couldn't help but feel a sense of excitement mixed with apprehension. They were stepping into uncharted territory, and there was no telling what dangers lay ahead.

Chapter Eight

The soft hum of computers and the glare of strip lighting filled the air in the offices of Paranormal Control, signalling the start of another nightshift. Ren sat poised at her desk. The glow of the computer screen cast a gentle illumination on her perplexed features, her brow furrowing as she studied the gruesome images in front of her. The horrific details of Lyndall Charwood's murder burned into her mind, haunting her as she tried to piece together the puzzle.

Having arrived early for her shift, alone in the office, Ren took a moment to lean back in her chair. She couldn't escape the eerie feeling that lingered as the ambient sounds of her own breathing mingled with the electronic buzz of the light directly above her.

Just as she was weighing up whether or not to make coffee, the office door burst open with a loud crash. Startled, her gaze snapped towards the entrance just as Amy strode in, her movements urgent and determined.

"I've been thinking," Amy said, slightly out of breath, "about last night, Erin, and the whole banshee theory. What if it's bullshit?"

"Go on," said Ren, sitting forward in her chair.

"Ok, so we know banshees burn in water, right? But if they actually killed Charwood – and indeed Redwood and Bundy – then why would they leave a body by the lake? It would be just as stupid as leaving a calling card. If a banshee committed a murder, and they can't go in water, then surely they would just dispose of the body somewhere else entirely? Like the woods or a dumpster?"

"That's a damn good point," Ren mused, her expression alight, inspired by Amy's theory. "Another paranormal could have committed the murders and left the bodies there to throw us off the scent."

"Exactly," said Amy. "And what if Erin was

lying when she mentioned her suspicions about the banshees?"

"But why would she lie?"

"Well, Erin has the Infernal Decadence mark on her palm, right? So that must mean she has some kind of loyalty to the club."

"Good point," said Ren. "I'm still not sure that I buy her story about the whole free drinks thing. I mean, a mark like that isn't something to be taken lightly. It's entirely possible that Erin knows a lot more than she's letting on."

"I agree."

"Erin mentioned that she's a regular at Infernal Decadence," Ren added. "We can always go there again to dig deeper."

"Yeah," said Amy. "If she's more loyal to Charles Bosgrove than she was letting on though, we might do better to go in a different direction."

"Such as?"

"What if we look for people who bear the Infernal Decadence mark, but wear it with regret instead of pride?" Amy suggested, a thoughtful expression on her face. "People who might have once been loyal, but now harbour doubts."

"It's a great idea," said Ren, "but how could we find someone who meets that criteria? It would be like looking for a needle in a haystack."

"Well," said Amy. "I'm not saying it would definitely work, but I think I've got an idea that's worth a shot: People often visit tattoo studios not just to get inked-up, but for advice on removing unwanted ink and paranormal marks. If we could find someone who regrets their mark and connection to Infernal Decadence, they might be more willing to talk openly about the club and Bosgrove."

Although Ren's scepticism still lingered a little, she couldn't help but feel inspired.

"If we could just find one person," she said, "they could be an excellent source of information."

"Someone who's been on the inside and is now willing to spill the truth," Amy said with a grin, pleased that her idea was taking shape.

Hours slipped by as they delved into the depths of social media groups and forums devoted solely to the tattoo culture of Emerald Heights. With dedicated fervour, they scoured every post and comment, seeking even a faint allusion to someone in need of a removal service for the Infernal Decadence mark. No matter how intently they searched though, their efforts proved fruitless, leaving them exasperated.

"Looks like we'll have to do this the old-fashioned way," Amy said with a sigh, rubbing her temples. "We'll hit up the local tattoo shops tomorrow and ask around."

"Ok," Ren replied, exhaustion weighing her down as she tried to stifle a yawn. "Let's call it a night. We'll have better luck when the tattoo studios are open during the day."

Demon Dusk

Chapter Nine

Sunlight peeked in through the curtains, casting a warm, golden glow on Ren's bedroom walls. Despite not having slept much, she forced herself to sit up and rub her eyes. Thoughts of Lyndall Charwood's case had swirled in her head like an unrelenting storm, refusing to let her rest. With a sigh, she swung her legs over the side of the bed and stood up, stretching her limbs and feeling the satisfying pops of her joints.

Damn, she thought, acknowledging for the millionth time how difficult it was to shut off her brain and practice self-care. Despite her years of experience as a Paranormal Control agent, the skill still eluded her.

She padded into the kitchen, barefoot and yawning, to make herself a strong cup of coffee. As the rich aroma filled her apartment, she couldn't help but smile. It was a small comfort, but one she welcomed nonetheless. Taking sips of the coffee in between getting dressed, she appreciated the stark hydration as its warmth and flavour awakened her senses.

Prepared for the day ahead, her body moving on autopilot whilst her mind continued to race, Ren stepped out of her apartment, locked the door, and activated the security system. She then made her way through the foyer and courtyard. To her delight, Amy was already waiting for her outside, a crisp red apple in hand and a bright smile on her face.

"Morning, sleepyhead," Amy teased, taking a bite of her apple as they began walking.

"Morning," said Ren. "So, tell me about this place we're going to."

"Ah, Sundays," Amy said, her face lighting up. "I've been going there for years. I got all my tattoos done by Fray Rossy, the owner. He's a straight-talking guy, and he's good at what he does. We've got a good rapport, so I'm hoping that he'll be ok to talk to us. Also, the studio is one of Emerald Heights' most popular tattoo places, so it seems like the best place to start."

"Sounds good," said Ren, eager to get some answers.

The city streets buzzed with life around them as they walked. The early morning air held a crisp vitality, stirring with the scent of breakfast from nearby cafés and the distant echoes of the daily awakening. Shop shutters creaked open, vendors arranged their wares, and the rhythmic hum of traffic shuddered from miles around. A sense of anticipation hung in the air, a brief interlude to the vibrance of a new day.

"There it is," said Amy, pointing to their destination that loomed ahead.

The tattoo studio, nestled between storefronts adorned with bold murals, signified the extent of the city's diverse clientele. Its exterior bore the intriguing signs of creative flair – a blend of graffiti-style artwork, expressive neon flyers, and a curated display of the studio's portfolio. Above all of that, was the studio's sign. A dazzling masterpiece against the clear morning sky, the lettering was in elegant, swirling script, each curve and loop seeming to reflect the illustrative stories waiting to be etched into the tapestry of skin. The bright hues of pink, indigo, and gold radiated with a lively energy that seemed to exude an abundance of expression.

The moment Ren and Amy stepped into Sundays, the tattoo studio announced itself as an inviting haven for art. Walls were covered in an eclectic mix of designs, from fierce dragons to delicate flowers, each piece a testament to the skilful hands that had brought them to life. The air held the subtle scent of disinfectant and ink, but it wasn't unpleasant.

"There he is," Amy said to Ren, motioning in the direction of the man at the reception counter.

Ren nodded as she took in the sight of the studio owner. She couldn't make out what he was working on, but his hands, calloused from years of craftsmanship, gracefully wielded a pen as he drew a seemingly complex design in a worn leather-bound sketchbook. His long black hair was tied back in a sleek ponytail, revealing his attractively expressive features.

"Hey, Fray!" Amy called out. "Have you got a minute?"

Fray looked up from his sketchbook, his face breaking into a wide grin when he saw Amy.

"Sure," he said, his voice a welcoming baritone, and his eyes twinkling with curiosity. "I hope I'm not in trouble!"

"Nothing like that," Amy assured him, a playful smirk on her lips. "We just need some information, and we think you might be able to help."

"Cool, ok," he said as he stepped out from behind the counter and extended a tattooed hand towards Ren. "Pleased to meet you. I'm Fray."

"Likewise," she replied, giving his hand a firm shake. "I'm Ren."

"My next client isn't due for an hour," Fray assured. "As long as the phone doesn't ring, you've got me all to yourselves."

"That's a relief," said Amy. "The questions we've got are of a sensitive nature."

"Ok, shoot," said Fray, looking unfazed.

"We're looking for someone who might have had the Infernal Decadence mark on their palm, but asked about having it removed," said Amy, getting straight to the point. "I know it's a long shot, but is there any chance that you've come across someone like that?"

Fray furrowed his brow, deep in thought. After a moment, his eyes widened.

"Actually, yeah," he said. "I've had not just one, but two people who have come in here to ask about getting their mark removed. One woman came in about a year ago, and another just three months back."

"Do you remember their names?" Ren asked keenly, her pulse quickening. "We'd really appreciate any information you could give us."

"Data protection doesn't apply when it comes to giving client information to Paranormal Control as part of an investigation," Amy

Chapter Nine

added. "And we can guarantee your protection if anything were to go wrong."

"Alright, I trust you," Fray said, loyalty in his gaze as he looked at Amy.

Moving behind the reception counter, he turned to his computer and scrolled through client records until he found the information.

"Here you go," he said. "Melissa Hegarty came in about a year ago, and Lyndall Charwood was here three months ago."

"Lyndall Charwood?!" Ren repeated, her heart pounding with excitement.

"Yeah," said Fray. "She was nice enough. She just popped in to make an enquiry. I've no idea if she went on to get her mark removed."

Ren gave Amy a knowing look, making it clear that now was the time to wrap things up.

"That's all we need for now," Amy told him, smiling gratefully. "We really appreciate your help."

"Anytime," said Fray. "It's no trouble at all."

"You'll see me again soon anyway," said Amy. "I'll be back in a few weeks for some more line work on my thigh."

"I'm looking forward to it," Fray said, grinning at Amy as he moved from behind the counter to get ready for his next client.

"Cheers, Fray," said Ren.

As Ren and Amy turned to leave the tattoo studio, a new sense of urgency gripped them both. They now had a vital lead to follow.

***

Ren and Amy stepped out of the tattoo studio, their minds buzzing over the new information. They walked briskly back to Paranormal Control, their steps echoing through the busy streets.

Propelled by haste, they entered the familiar building and whisked through the corridors and bustling office. The clamour of activity seemed to hush around them as they reached a private meeting room, quickly closing the

Chapter Nine

door behind them and keen to discuss their new lead.

"Can you believe it?" Amy said, enthusiastically taking a seat. "Lyndall Charwood wanted to get rid of the mark. Something must have happened that made her want to sever ties with Infernal Decadence."

"Indeed," said Ren, alert and still on her feet. "We need to find Melissa Hegarty. If she's gone through something similar with Infernal Decadence, then maybe she can shed some light on what's going on there."

She quickly sat down in front of a computer, her fingers flying across the keyboard as she searched online for a Melissa Hegarty.

"Nothing," she muttered, frustration edging her voice. "There doesn't seem to be a single person in Emerald Heights with that name."

"Wait, look at this," Amy said, pointing to an entry on Ren's screen. "There's a Melissa Hegarty living on a farm called Rooster's Keep. That's about seventy miles from here."

"It could be a different person," Ren mused, pausing to chew on her lip. "But I guess it's our best bet at the moment."

"Exactly," Amy agreed. "And if it's the Melissa Hegarty that we're looking for, she could have all kinds of useful information."

Ren couldn't help but feel a surge of adrenaline at the thought of uncovering the truth behind Lyndall Charwood's murder.

"Alright," she said, determination setting her jaw. "We'll head out to Rooster's Keep this afternoon."

Chapter Ten

A soft, warm breeze blew through Ren's pink hair as she stepped out of the unmarked car and surveyed the picturesque scene before her. Rooster's Keep was like a painting come to life. With its rolling green hills, vibrant flowerbeds, and quaint farm buildings nestled under a vast, cloudless sky, it exuded a soothing air of tranquillity.

Amy exited from the other side of the car, stretching her tattooed arms above her head before taking in the same idyllic landscape.

"Damn, I could get used to this," she muttered, her eyes scanning the farm with an appreciative gleam.

"It's like a different world compared to the city," said Ren.

As they stood there, the distant sound of laughter reached their ears, drawing their attention to a group of people gathered nearby.

"It looks like some sort of tour," Amy said quietly.

"Yeah," Ren agreed, her gaze locking onto the young woman standing and facing the group.

With their curiosity piqued, Ren and Amy exchanged glances before making their way along the cobbled path towards the assembly of people. They then slipped into the group, careful not to draw attention to themselves as they hung back and observed the young woman leading what appeared to be a tour of the farm. She seemed to be in her early twenties, her face alight with enthusiasm as she spoke passionately about chickens. Her audience hung on her every word, captivated by her knowledge and genuine love for the animals in her care.

"Did you know that chickens can recognise up to a hundred different faces?" she asked her admiring audience, her expression radiant with excitement. "Not just human

Chapter Ten

faces, but other chickens too!"

"Wow, that's impressive," Amy whispered under her breath, glancing over at Ren who nodded in agreement.

"Alright, folks, I think that's enough chicken trivia for one day," the young woman announced cheerfully. "Feel free to head over to our gift shop and check out some of our farm-fresh products."

As the group dispersed, Ren and Amy lingered behind, waiting for the perfect moment to approach the sweet-faced woman. When she bent down to gently stroke a hen, Ren cleared her throat and stepped forward.

"Excuse me," she began cautiously, not wanting to startle her. "We really enjoyed your talk about the chickens. It's clear you care a lot about them."

"Thanks," said the woman, clearly appreciative of the praise as she gave a warm smile. "I love my little feathered friends. They're so much more interesting than people give them credit for."

"I agree," Amy chimed in, her tattooed arms folding across her chest as she offered an encouraging nod. "By the way, we were wondering if you know anyone named Melissa Hegarty around here?"

"Melissa? Yeah, she's my sister. I'm Charlie Hegarty."

"Nice to meet you, Charlie," said Ren. "I'm Ren, and this is Amy. Do you think we could talk to Melissa?"

"Of course," Charlie replied, her voice betraying a hint of concern. "Is everything ok?"

"There's nothing to worry about," Ren assured, even as her thoughts raced with the urgency of their mission. "We just need to ask her a few questions."

"She's in the house right now," Charlie said cautiously.

"Have either of you ever lived in Emerald Heights?" Ren asked gently, highly aware that she needed to tread carefully.

Chapter Ten

Charlie's face fell at the mention of Emerald Heights.

"Yes," she said, her voice trembling as she answered. "We used to live there, but we left about a year ago."

"We don't mean any harm," Ren said quickly before lowering her voice. "We're from Paranormal Control. We need to speak with Melissa about Infernal Decadence."

The mention of Infernal Decadence seemed to pierce Charlie's heart, her shoulders tensing as she struggled to maintain her composure. The topic was clearly a sore one.

"Please, we just want to help," Amy added, her sincerity shining through.

"Alright," Charlie conceded. "Follow me."

Ren and Amy followed Charlie's lead. She took them along a stony path that meandered through the farm, past various barns and patches of wildflowers. The farmhouse emerged like a postcard scene from another era, its timeworn wooden exterior adorned with climbing ivy. A picket fence surrounded the property, its white paint weathered, but steadfast in delineating a sanctuary from the wild expanse beyond.

They then followed Charlie up the cobbled pathway and watched as she swung open the door of the farmhouse, revealing the warm, inviting interior. Sunlight streamed in through the windows, casting a golden glow on the polished wooden floors and rustic furniture. The scent of freshly-baked bread wafted from the kitchen, mingling with the faint aroma of lavender.

"Melissa!" Charlie called out, her voice slightly strained. "There are two women here who'd like to speak with you."

Ren and Amy exchanged glances, tensing as they waited for Melissa's response. A moment later, a woman emerged from the kitchen. She had an apron tied around her waist and a dusting of flour on her hands. She patted them together, sending a small cloud of white powder into the air. As she did so, Ren quickly observed that there were no markings on either of her palms.

"Can I help you?" Melissa asked warily, eyeing

Chapter Ten

the two strangers in her home.

"Hi," said Ren, showing her identity badge with a firm confidence. "I'm Ren Cain, and this is my colleague – Amy Carver. We're from Paranormal Control. We'd like to talk to you about your time in Emerald Heights."

"You're not in any trouble," Amy quickly added. "Far from it."

Melissa sighed heavily, but seemed to sense that she could talk to the two women in front of her.

"Please, have a seat," she said as she walked Ren and Amy through to the lounge.

She gestured towards the plush sofa on the edge of the cosy space. Ren and Amy sat down, taking in the room's comforting atmosphere – the family photos adorning the walls, the soft blankets draped over the backs of chairs, and the homemade knickknacks scattered about. It contrasted starkly with the dark tone of what they were about to discuss.

Melissa sat down in an armchair facing Ren and Amy, nervously ready to listen.

"Melissa," Ren began, her voice firm but gentle. "We believe you used to be associated with Infernal Decadence, and we want to find out more."

The mention of Infernal Decadence seemed to stab at Melissa's heart. Her breath hitched, and her hands twisted anxiously in her lap.

"Take your time," Amy said softly. "You're not in any trouble."

"Charles was just so... captivating," Melissa said, her voice barely a whisper. "I thought he really cared about me, you know? But I was just a fool."

As she looked to Ren and Amy for understanding, her eyes brimmed with unshed tears.

"Charles Bosgrove?" Ren asked. "The club owner?"

"Yeah," Melissa confirmed. "He'd take me to all these fancy parties, introducing me to important people. He made me feel special, like I belonged in his world, and like he cared about me."

Chapter Ten

As a bitter laugh escaped her lips, the hurt in her eyes spoke volumes.

"It's ok," said Amy. "Take your time."

"I overheard him one night," Melissa continued, wiping her eyes with the back of her hand. "He was talking to some guy about how much he could make off me. From that moment, it hit me that I was just another pretty face for sale – nothing more than a pawn in one of his so-called business ventures."

"That must have been awful for you," said Ren.

"It was," said Melissa. "From that point on, I wanted nothing to do with Charles. He's a sick, arrogant man. The next day, I went straight to Sundays tattoo studio. The owner there was brilliant. He put me in touch with someone who could remove the Infernal Decadence mark from my palm. Charles had given it to me when we started dating. He made me feel special, but once I'd seen his true colours, I couldn't stand to look at it."

"So you got the mark removed?" said Ren.

"That should have been the end of it, right?"

"I thought so too," said Melissa, her voice shaking with emotion. "When I told Charles what I'd done, and told him that we were over, he shoved me against the wall, put his hand around my neck, and threatened to kill me. I knew right there and then that I was no longer safe in Emerald Heights."

"And that's why you're now here?" said Amy, gesturing to the room around them.

"That's right," Melissa confirmed, her voice becoming steadier. "Best decision I ever made. Charles is a coward. He's too wrapped up in his business with Infernal Decadence to be of any concern to me now. I know that for him, I'm out of sight and out of mind. He's got so many other women under his thumb that his main focus is keeping them in line. Out here, I'm old news to him, thank fuck."

"Well," said Ren, passing Melissa her contact details. "If you ever feel differently about that and want to request protection, you only have to ask."

"Thanks," said Melissa, her tone laced with

relief. "I appreciate it."

"You might not know the answer to this," Amy said thoughtfully, "but is it only non-paranormals that Charles gets involved with?"

"You mean in terms of the women he recruits?" Melissa asked.

Ren and Amy both nodded their heads.

"Yeah," Melissa said confidently. "As I said, Charles is a coward. He recruits non-paranormals and relies on his demonic charisma – not only to attract people, but to keep them in line. He's a bastard. I'm glad to be out of it."

"Well," said Ren, "you've got our number if you need anything. We really appreciate the information you've given us."

"Thanks," said Melissa.

Ren and Amy rose from their seats, the soft creak of the lounge furniture echoing the transition from questions to gratitude. As they made their way towards the door,

Melissa accompanied them.

"Take care, both of you," she said. "If you're going to bring that bastard down, you have my full support."

Chapter Eleven

A beam of sunlight filtered in through the partially-opened blinds, casting long, slanted shadows across the industrial carpeting of the private office. Ren and Amy sat before Brent Statham, their shoulders tense and their expressions serious as they finished recounting every detail of their meticulous investigation into Lyndall Charwood's murder.

"Excellent work, both of you," Statham said, his voice authoritative but encouraging as he leaned back in his chair. "The intel you've gathered is compelling, to say the least. I agree that it's time we tighten our surveillance on Charles Bosgrove. He's become a key suspect in this case."

"Ok, so hear me out," said Amy, enthusiastically leaning forward in her chair.

"What if we go undercover as women that Bosgrove would want for his entourage? We could get closer to him and find out more about his operation."

Ren raised an eyebrow, impressed by Amy's bold suggestion.

"I second that," she said. "We can't deny the dangers of getting that close to Bosgrove, but it might just work."

Statham's expression shifted to one of doubt as he rubbed his stubbled chin thoughtfully. With a deep frown, he finally shook his head in disagreement.

"I appreciate your dedication," he said respectfully, "but I can't condone such a high-risk approach."

"Sir," Ren protested, her voice laced with frustration. "We can handle ourselves. It could be our best shot at getting the intel we need."

"Even if I were to allow it, there's no guarantee that you'd be able to infiltrate Bosgrove's inner circle," Statham countered, his tone firm. "Your evidence suggests that he's an influential and powerful individual. There's a vital line to be drawn between surveillance and getting too close to someone like that."

"Then what do you suggest?" Amy asked, folding her arms defensively.

"Based on the information you've gathered, I believe there's enough evidence to warrant the use of a tracking device on one of Bosgrove's associates," Statham replied, meeting their surprised gazes. "It's not a decision I take lightly, but considering the gravity of the situation, it's necessary."

"A tracking device?" Ren questioned, her tone rising in surprise. "Isn't that supposed to be a last resort?"

"Normally, yes," Statham admitted. "But we need to tread carefully with Bosgrove. The last thing we want is to tip him off and send him into hiding."

"Alright, what if we go back to Infernal Decadence and put a tracking device on Erin?" Ren suggested. "She's got that mark on her palm, so she's clearly connected to Bosgrove in some way. If she's one of the women working for him, she could be a goldmine of information."

Statham considered the proposition, his steely gaze giving nothing away. After a moment of contemplation, he gave a single nod, indicating his agreement with a subtle yet decisive gesture.

"It's risky, but it could work," he said. "Just make sure you stay under the radar while you're there. We can't risk alerting Bosgrove to our presence."

"Understood," Amy chimed in, sharing a determined glance with Ren. "We'll get in, plant the tracker, and get out without raising any suspicions."

"Good," Statham said, sitting forward in his chair as he regarded them both with a resolute expression. "And remember: your safety comes first. If things go south, don't hesitate to pull out. I don't want either of you getting hurt over this."

"Thanks, Sir," Ren replied, an appreciative

Chapter Eleven

smile tugging at the corners of her mouth. "We won't let you down."

With that, Ren and Amy left the office, their minds racing for the mission ahead. Ren couldn't help but feel the weight of responsibility pressing down on her shoulders. They had come so far in their investigation, and now everything hinged on their ability to plant a tracking device on Erin without being discovered.

"Hey," Amy said softly. "Are you ok?"

"Of course," Ren replied, forcing a smile. "I'm just… thinking about the plan."

"Me too," Amy admitted, her expression serious. "But we've got this, Ren. We're going to nail this."

"Damn right we are," Ren agreed, her confidence bolstered by Amy's unwavering faith in their abilities.

Demon Dusk

Chapter Twelve

The throbbing bass of Infernal Decadence reverberated through the soles of Ren's boots, each beat syncing with the pounding in her chest. Demons and non-paranormals alike swayed and gyrated to the relentless rhythm, their frenzied movements casting eerie shadows beneath the harsh glare of the strobe lights.

Ren looked at Amy and shook her head, communicating that she hadn't caught sight of Erin yet. Amy rhythmically bobbed her head in understanding, expertly feigning some quirky dance moves as she maintained her own watch over the area.

In the hot nightclub, Ren swiped at the beads of sweat trickling down her temples, leaving streaks of pink hair plastered to her forehead. It was an effort to suppress her irritation as she scanned the sea of revellers around them.

She was desperate to catch a glimpse of Erin's telltale green hair. As she scanned the area, the club's relentless beat seeped into her bones, pulsing in time with her mounting frustration. Amy caught Ren's attention with a shake of her head, confirming what they already knew: their target remained elusive.

Damn it, Ren thought, feeling the responsibility of their mission bearing down on her. There was so much at stake. With every passing second, she could feel the room closing in on her, the frenzied energy of the crowd threatening to swallow her whole.

Focus, she reminded herself, clenching her fists at her sides. She couldn't let her emotions get in the way now.

She chewed her lip, trying to keep her cool, her gaze darting from one face to another as she searched for Erin. As the night continued with no luck, an uneasy feeling settled in her gut.

"I'm going to head upstairs," she spoke clearly into Amy's ear, raising her voice to be heard

Chapter Twelve

above the domineering music. "Perhaps the smoking area is where it's at."

Amy nodded, her eyes filled with determination as she moved to the relentless beat.

As Ren pushed her way through the crowd, she couldn't help but feel as though she was swimming against the current, fighting to stay afloat amidst the chaos.

She headed up the stairs out of the underground nightclub. The air becoming cooler, and the music becoming slightly muted, it gave her a moment to take a breath and clear her head.

As she emerged at ground level, the stark contrast between the stifling heat of the club and the cold outside sent shivers down her spine. She pulled her leather jacket tighter around her body, steeling herself for a long night.

The quiet streets were a world away from the hectic energy of the dance floor. Streetlights painted the pavement in hues of deep peach and pale lemon, casting an otherworldly glow that seemed to soothe the city's after-hours canvas. The faraway hum of receding traffic echoed on the waves of a distant breeze.

As Ren surveyed the nocturnal landscape, she couldn't shake the feeling that the unease of the recent murders still lingered on the consciousness of every young woman in the city. Everyone was a potential victim until the murderer could be found and brought to justice.

All of a sudden, a flash of green caught Ren's attention as a woman burst out of an alleyway, her movements driven by panic and urgency.

That's Erin!

Adrenaline surged through Ren's veins as she launched into a full sprint. Her heart pounded in her ears, drowning out everything but the sound of her own breathing and the clapping of her boots against the pavement.

Fuck, she's fast!

Gritting her teeth, Ren doggedly pursued

Chapter Twelve

Erin through the city streets. The relentless chase took her past darkened storefronts and beneath countless streetlights, the shadows seeming to reach out and grasp at her with every step she took.

She knew that losing sight of Erin wasn't an option. She followed after her with no regard for her own exhaustion, her resolve unwavering despite the painful ache in her muscles.

Suddenly, Erin darted around a corner and charged into a shadowy alleyway, leaving Ren with no sight of her.

In the dead end, there was nowhere for Erin to run. As Ren took her first steps into the alley, her breath caught in her throat as she took in the sight of her target.

Huddled against a graffiti-covered wall, Erin was in a state of distress. Her once-luscious green hair hung in tangled strands. Tear tracks stained her dirt-smudged cheeks, mixing with the remnants of dried blood that was caked around her nostrils. Her face was a canvas of bruises, each one telling its own painful story. Her body trembled as she sobbed uncontrollably, humiliated and afraid.

"Erin!" Ren exclaimed breathily, rushing to her side. "What happened? Who did this to you?"

"Bosgrove set me up with a shit of a client," Erin choked out between sobs, her eyes brimming with anger and fear.

"Shit," said Ren, clenching her fists, her nails digging into her palms as rage boiled beneath her skin.

Although Ren was enthused and motivated about the intel the situation was providing, she couldn't help but be furious about what Erin must have gone through; she was clearly being exploited.

"Where's Bosgrove now?" Ren demanded, her voice low and dangerous.

"I don't know," said Erin, her fingers trembling as she wiped away fresh tears. "I last saw him in that alley when he told me to... take care of his client. But the client... he was so rough... I couldn't..."

Chapter Twelve

The raw pain in Erin's voice hit Ren like a punch to the gut. This was it: the proof they needed that Bosgrove was manipulating these young women, using them for his own twisted purposes. It was time to make a move.

"Listen, Erin," Ren said firmly, her eyes locking onto the younger woman's. "I'm not just some clubber. I'm with Paranormal Control. We can help you press charges against Bosgrove if you work with us."

"But what about Lyndall, Samantha, and Candice?" Erin asked, her voice tainted by a deep-seated terror. "I don't want to end up like them."

"Those women were killed by banshees, right?" Ren asked, trying to keep her tone neutral.

"That's just what I was told to say to anyone who would listen," Erin admitted, her voice shaking.

"Erin, we can protect you," Ren promised, sincerity in her words. "Come with me back to headquarters, and we'll make sure you're safe."

"Ok," said Erin, her resolve hardening. "I'll do it."

Ren gave a reassuring smile, and then pulled out her phone to send a quick text to Amy. She had barely hit send when an ear-piercing scream tore through the air, causing her heart to leap into her throat.

"Ren!" Erin shrieked, her eyes wide with alarm. "Look!"

Ren turned around. There, at the mouth of the alley, stood Charles Bosgrove, his predatory gaze fixed on her as he stalked towards them. A sick feeling washed over Ren as it dawned on her that she'd been followed. Her only option now was to face this bastard head-on.

"Run, Erin!" she shouted, a surge of panic in her voice. "Get out of here!"

As Erin scrambled to get away, Ren braced herself.

Chapter Thirteen

The cold wind whistled through the dark alleyway, causing Ren to shudder as she stared into the menacing eyes of Charles Bosgrove. The dim glow from a flickering streetlight cast eerie shadows onto his face, emphasising his demonic features. Dressed in a navy pinstripe suit and a white shirt with a large collar that left the top of his muscular chest exposed to the elements, he took one last puff of his cigar and threw the rest of it down on the ground, crushing it with a polished boot whilst never taking his gaze off Ren for even a second.

"I'll make sure you never breathe a word of this to anyone," he said with a sneer, his voice as smooth as silk, but dripping with malice.

Without warning, he lunged forward, his supernatural strength propelling him at high speed. Ren ducked just in time, feeling the rush of air as a clawed hand swiped at where her head had been moments before. She countered with a swift kick to his side, but he didn't so much as flinch.

"Is that all you've got?" he taunted, a sinister grin spreading across his face. "This will be easier than I thought."

Ren winced, her hair whipping around her face as she tried to ignore the fear that threatened to paralyse her. She couldn't let Bosgrove win – not after everything she'd been through to keep Emerald Heights safe from demons like him.

How the hell am I supposed to beat someone so powerful? she thought, her mind racing as she searched for a weakness.

"Surely you've got *something* in that pretty little head of yours," Bosgrove mocked, rolling his shoulders with an almost lazy confidence. "And there I was thinking that you'd have a little more fight in you than the likes of poor young Lyndall – and the useless ones before her: Samantha and Candice."

Chapter Thirteen

He killed them!

Taking great delight in how his words unnerved her, Bosgrove flashed a condescending smile at Ren, causing her to recoil at the sharpness of his tobacco-stained teeth. Her breath escaped in short, sharp bursts. She knew she was outmatched, but there had to be *something* she could use against him. Her eyes darted around the alleyway, searching for anything that could give her an edge.

"Looking for help?" he said, his tone laced with sadistic amusement. "You won't find it here."

With a languid grace, the demon advanced, each step deliberate, a malevolent ballet choreographed to amplify Ren's sense of entrapment as he left her with no choice but to back away from him and towards the certain dead end of a high wall. His moves were not a mere tactical approach, but a macabre dance of intimidation.

To Ren, the demon's proximity was not solely physical; it was an intrusion into the very recesses of her psyche, a calculated invasion meant to unravel her resolve. The walls of the alley seemed to close in on her, the very air thrumming with the tension. Bosgrove appeared to be enjoying every moment of this, like a spider relishing the vulnerability of its captive prey, his every word a taunting melody, resonating with calculated cruelty.

"Fuck you," Ren said angrily, her breath coming in ragged gasps as she struggled to stay on the offensive.

It was becoming increasingly clear that she needed to find a new approach if she was to stand a chance against him. Still though, if there was one thing she'd learnt during her time as a Paranormal Control agent, it was that sometimes sheer willpower could trump even the most overwhelming odds.

Refusing to abandon her search for a solution, Ren suddenly spotted an empty glass bottle nestled amongst a pile of discarded takeaway boxes. With no time to waste, she lunged for it and then smashed it against the wall, turning it into a makeshift weapon. The jagged shards glinted in the dim light, reflecting her determination back at her.

Chapter Thirteen

"Ah, you're getting creative!" Bosgrove taunted as he took another step forward, his exceptional height now almost towering over Ren.

I won't let this piece of shit intimidate me.

Ren prepared to focus all her energy on her next move. Before she could strike though, Bosgrove closed the distance between them with supernatural speed, his eyes blazing with unholy glee. As he raised his hand in readiness for a lethal strike, Ren could almost feel the razor-sharp claws slicing through her flesh, carving an irreversible path to her end.

"Any last words, sweetheart?" he said, smirking as his voice dripped with venom.

"Go to hell," Ren snapped defiantly as she struggled to keep her fear at bay.

"Already been there, darling," Bosgrove replied, his confidence only growing as he sensed the vulnerability of his target. "Now, be a good girl, and die."

Ren tightened her grip around the cold, hard bottle neck in her hand, her knuckles turning white with the effort. She refused to give this smug bastard the satisfaction of taking her down without a fight.

As much as she hoped that Bosgrove would back down, something in the back of her mind warned her that he wouldn't. With lightning-fast speed, he brought his hand down to strike her, and although she managed to parry the attack, she felt helpless, her grip still desperately on her makeshift weapon. As primitive as it was, she knew that without it, she would be as good as dead. Never had she been faced with someone as monstrous and as calculating as Bosgrove.

Her bravado was starting to wear thin; she knew that Bosgrove would soon break through her defences. Her pulse raced as she prepared herself for the end. As the cold wind whipped at her pink hair, the dirty scent of the alleyway filled her nostrils – a fittingly harsh backdrop for her final moments.

"Never mind," Bosgrove said darkly, his clawed hand poised to deliver a deathly blow. "Nobody lives forever."

Chapter Thirteen

Ren squeezed her eyes shut, her thoughts a maelstrom of regret and anger. She should have been more careful. She should have seen this coming. But it was too late now – all she could do was hope that Amy would bring Bosgrove to justice without her.

"Leave her alone, you bastard!" a loud female voice suddenly ordered from the entrance of the alleyway, shattering the eerie moment that had settled over them.

Ren's eyes shot open just in time to see Bosgrove freeze, his clawed hand suspended above her head, and his demonic visage contorting with surprise. A surge of hope coursed through her veins as she spotted Amy; standing defiantly at the mouth of the alley, her tattooed arms wielded a gun that was aimed directly at Bosgrove's head. The weapon gleamed menacingly in the dim light, a beacon of hope and defiance.

"You think you're invincible, don't you?" Amy challenged, her grip on the gun unwavering. "Dream on, you piece of shit."

"Your loyalty is touching," Bosgrove replied, his smile returning as he took a step back from Ren. "But ultimately, it's pointless."

"Get away from her," Amy ordered, the steel in her voice leaving no room for doubt. "Or I'll blow your fucking brains out."

Not cocky enough to push his luck entirely, Bosgrove complied and took another step back. Ren seized the moment to push off from the cold brick wall.

"Ren, now!" Amy shouted, her voice laced with urgency.

The command resonated within Ren like a war cry, igniting a fire deep within her soul. She sprang forward towards Bosgrove, closing the distance between them before swiftly extending her trembling arm and driving the shattered glass bottle firmly into his exposed chest. The jagged edges tore through his flesh, ripping and shredding as she twisted the bottle, images of his victims flashing through her mind. She felt the vicious shards reach his heart with a sickening crunch.

The demon let out a guttural scream as blood seeped out of him and dribbled down his torso in rivers of crimson. Ren stood frozen, watching as he staggered back, his once-proud and intimidating form now hunched over in agony. Every muscle in his body seemed to be straining against an invisible force, the pain etched into every line of his face.

"Die, you bastard!" Ren shouted, still in a state of shock.

Bosgrove emitted another unearthly scream, a primitive wail that bounced off the walls of the alley. His eyes widened with disbelief as he looked down to see the blood flowing freely from his heart, staining his once-pristine shirt a sinister shade of red.

Ren's breath caught in her throat as she watched the life drain from her target. His body jerked and twisted in its final violent throes before shrinking and disintegrating into a small mound of ash on the ground, leaving behind only a faint trail of dust rising towards the moonlit sky. The demon's once-powerful figure was now nothing more than mere remnants and memories.

Despite the necessity of Bosgrove's demise, a

sense of disgust churned in Ren's stomach as she stood there, stunned. The sight of the disintegrating demon had been both awe-inspiring and revolting. She couldn't tear her gaze away, even as the acrid smell of sulphur filled her nose and caught in her throat.

As a gentle breeze blew through the narrow space, it became clear that the pile of ashes wouldn't stay in place for long, a testament to the fact that the battle was truly over. The sight served to colour Ren's sense of triumph, a feeling that this was a victory hard-won and well-deserved.

"Fuck, that was close," Ren said breathily, her heart still hammering in her chest.

She glanced over at Amy, who had lowered the gun and was surveying the aftermath with a mixture of relief and apprehension.

"Too close," Amy agreed, visibly trembling from the adrenaline rush.

"Thank fuck you got here – and just in time! How did you find me?"

"I bumped into Erin as she was fleeing from

Chapter Thirteen

here. She told me where to find you."

"Shit," Ren muttered. "Is she ok?"

"She seemed more terrified than hurt, but I'll see to it that we look after her," Amy said. "I told her I was Paranormal Control and on her side. Poor girl looked like she'd seen a ghost."

"Where is she now?"

"I told her to wait for us. She's in the back of an unmarked car."

"Good move," said Ren. "We'll take her back to headquarters. Not only do we need to get a statement from her, but we need to make sure she gets the support she needs."

In that moment, Ren suddenly succumbed to her own feelings of vulnerability. As much as she had tried to hold them back, the threshold broke and tears began to fall down her cheeks, carving a raw, unfiltered path through the mask she usually wore.

"Hey, hey... it's ok," Amy said gently as she took Ren into a soothing embrace of camaraderie. "You've been so brave tonight.

I'm proud of you. I'm proud of *us*. Let's get back to headquarters and make sure that we all get the aftercare we need. It's been one hell of a night."

Chapter Fourteen

The harsh office strip lights of Paranormal Control cast a stark and unforgiving shine on the blood splattered across Ren's black leather jacket. Breathing heavily, she leaned against her desk, her pink hair clinging to her sweat-streaked forehead. Her fingers trembled as she whipped out her phone and dialled Statham's out-of-hours number.

"I know it's late, Sir, but this is an emergency," she said frankly, the weight of the night's events hanging heavily on her words. "We need you to come in right away."

"Alright, I'm on my way," Statham confirmed.

Ren ended the call and put her phone in her pocket, relieved that her boss could sense the imperative nature of the situation.

"Is he coming?" Amy asked as she stood protectively beside Erin.

"Yeah," Ren muttered, rubbing at her throbbing temples. "I've no idea what his reaction will be."

"We did what we had to do, Ren," Amy said gently.

"Thanks," Ren murmured, managing a weak smile.

She knew Amy would have her back no matter what, but it was still comforting to hear it out loud. A thousand thoughts raced through her mind as she replayed the altercation in the alley. Deep down, she knew they had done the right thing, but it was still shocking nevertheless.

"Erin," Ren said, her tone caring but firm. "We're going to need a statement from you, about everything that's happened tonight. But first, get yourself cleaned up, alright?"

"Thanks," Erin said gratefully. "I don't know what I would have done without you two. I think I'm still in shock."

Chapter Fourteen

"You must be," said Ren. "It's natural. I think we all are."

"Come on," said Amy, offering a kind smile to Erin. "I'll show you where the showers are."

She guided Erin out of the room, leaving Ren alone in the quiet office.

As Ren waited for Statham to arrive, she paced back and forth. She couldn't settle. She couldn't shake the image of Bosgrove's twisted, agonised expressions, or the way his blood had felt warm and sticky on her hands. It made her stomach churn, but she knew she'd done what was necessary. Nobody else would have to suffer his cruelty now.

Trying to steady her thoughts, Ren ran a hand through her pink hair. It was still damp with sweat, and her black leather jacket felt too heavy, suffocating even. She shrugged it off and tossed it onto a nearby chair before sinking into another one herself.

Leaning back, she allowed herself a moment of vulnerability, closing her eyes and pressing the heels of her hands to her temples, massaging them more firmly than before. So many conflicting emotions swirled within her.

Although the office door opened with a quiet click, the sound caused Ren's heart to leap in her chest. Statham strode in, his face an unreadable mask of concern and authority.

"Ren," he said, his voice clipped with haste. "I got here as fast as I could. What's happened?"

"Take a seat, Sir," she said. "It's a long story."

Ren gestured to the chair opposite her, trying to keep her composure as she braced herself for the retelling. Statham sat down, his gaze never leaving her face.

"Charles Bosgrove admitted to the murders," she began, her knuckles turning white as she gripped the edge of her chair. "He confessed everything to me before he attacked. We fought in the alley. I had to kill him, Sir. It was him or me."

Statham's expression remained impassive, but there was a flicker of something in his eyes – maybe pity, maybe understanding. Ren couldn't be sure. She took a deep breath

Chapter Fourteen

and carried on.

"Amy was brilliant," she said fiercely, the words tumbling out of her almost too quickly to understand. "She threatened to shoot Bosgrove, and that distraction allowed me to drive a broken glass bottle into his heart. He didn't stand a chance after that."

"It sounds like you both did what you had to do," Statham said evenly, his gaze still locked on Ren's face. "We can't afford to take chances when it comes to demons like Bosgrove."

"Did I just hear you talking me up?" Amy teased, emerging from the corridor with a freshly-showered Erin following behind.

A playful smirk tugged at the corner of Amy's mouth despite the fatigue evident in her posture.

"Damn right," Ren replied. "You were fearless out there."

Erin nodded vigorously, her damp green hair swaying with the motion.

"You two saved my life," she said. "I can't thank you enough."

"You're more than welcome," Statham asserted. "It pains me to think that you could have been Bosgrove's next victim."

Erin winced. The severity of the situation was all too stark.

"I want you both to know that I support your actions completely," Statham said to Ren and Amy, his expression resolute. "Not only did you have no choice but to defend yourselves, but you did what you had to do to protect the people of this city, and for that, I commend you."

Ren glanced over at Amy, who rolled her shoulders back, seeming to stand taller under Statham's praise.

"Thank you," Amy said, her voice steady and filled with gratitude.

Statham then turned to address Erin.

"Erin," he said, "I want you to know that after you've made your statement, Paranormal

Chapter Fourteen

Control has got your back. If there's anything you need in terms of protection, you have only to ask."

"Thank you," she replied.

"Will you feel safe going home alone after everything that's happened?"

Erin took a moment to think, her eyes narrowing as she considered the question.

"Yeah," she said eventually. "I don't think there's anything to be scared of now. I know Bosgrove was working alone, and now that he's dead, no henchmen will care to work for him anymore. He won't be around to pay them. They only liked him for his money. He'd charm women into working for him, and then intimidate them when they saw his true colours and wanted out. Yeah, now that Bosgrove's dead, there's nothing to fear."

Ren bit her lip, mulling over Erin's words. They came as a major relief; the thought of anyone else being targeted had been weighing heavily on her mind.

"Alright," said Statham. "Once you've given

your statement, we'll take you home."

"Thank you," said Erin, her expression one of relief.

Epilogue

In the weeks that followed Charles Bosgrove being brought to justice, life in Emerald Heights underwent a transformation, each thread of the city's tapestry weaving a tale of resolution and renewal.

Despite how Infernal Decadence had thrived under the corrupt ownership of Bosgrove, its popularity, and client demand, was undeniable – so much so, that a buyer stepped up at the last hour, saving the venue from closure. Now though, it would no longer serve as a façade to conceal a reign of crime and exploitation. Taking an active role in preserving the desirable aspects of the underground nightclub, the new owner ushered in a new era for the supernatural hotspot. The once-malevolent undertones of the club morphed into a haven for those wishing to embrace its mysterious but non-threatening allure.

Happy to have helped Ren and Amy in their investigation, Fray Rossy pointed Erin – and the other women who had been under Bosgrove's thumb – in the direction of a paranormal mark removal specialist. Everyone welcomed the opportunity to get the Infernal Decadence mark removed from their palm, for although the nightclub itself was respected, everyone was now free to be their own person. No longer did they have to pledge loyalty to a demon who sought to exploit them. In breaking the chains that bound them to the sinister connection, the women found solace in the removal of their unwanted symbols, reclaiming their autonomy in a gesture that spoke of empowerment born from adversity.

Erin, having found the support she needed from friends, family, and other victims, immersed herself in her studies. Profusely apologising to the banshees and advocating for their goodness, although it took time and continued effort, she mended the fractured bonds of trust. The banshees, having completed their exchange programme at the university, bid farewell to Emerald Heights, their ethereal songs immortalised in the memories of those who had crossed their paths.

The site of Lake Seraphim held no more secrets. Families of the victims, though traumatised from everything they had endured, found a semblance of comfort in justice served. With the city extending a collective support network, those who had suffered loss were offered ongoing help in their continued grief.

The ever-popular Rooster's Keep continued to thrive under the ownership of the Hegarty sisters. Charlie continued to run tours of the farm, sharing her passion and expertise for the animals, whilst Melissa threw herself into growing the rural haven into a thriving business. Although she still bore the emotional scars of her time in Emerald Heights, the news of Bosgrove's demise helped to ease her pain significantly. She made sure to phone Ren and Amy to personally thank them.

In recognition of Ren and Amy's hard work on such a challenging case, Brent Statham issued a resolute directive: two weeks off. Despite initial resistance from Ren, a relaxing spa day marked the beginning of her well-deserved hiatus. Amy made sure to tell Ren that self-care was no longer optional, and Ren promised to embrace that philosophy whilst on holiday at a luxurious winter resort.

Before jetting off on her own holiday, Amy made sure to visit Sundays. Fray did a wonderful job of the line work on her thigh. Keeping her new art covered as it healed, Amy didn't let it stop her from soaking up the sun as she embraced the relaxing delights of the beach.

Charles Bosgrove, his name once whispered with fear, became a forgotten echo in the annals of Emerald Heights' history. His fair-weather entourage, like scattered leaves in the wind, dissipated, leaving the memory of the demon's dark influence to be overshadowed by the emergence of a city reborn from his corruption.

Bathed in the glow of hope and optimism, Emerald Heights faced the dawn of a new chapter, leaving behind the shadows of Bosgrove's tyranny. And whilst the city would forever be vulnerable to the clandestine manoeuvres of unscrupulous paranormals, Paranormal Control, in their unyielding commitment, would remain steadfast guardians, their efforts eternally invested in protecting each and every citizen.

Demon Dusk

Milton Keynes UK
Ingram Content Group UK Ltd.
UKHW010900080524
442402UK00004B/96